Collins

THE NAME IS KADE

Alan Gibbons and Robbie Gibbons

Illustrated by
Eoin Coveney

CHAPTER 1

The name is Kade, Jack Kade. I take the jobs the cops can't do. I clear the skyways of the scum of the universe. I hunt down the gangsters, the kidnappers, every kind of low life. It's a dirty job, but somebody has to do it.

I get my orders from the top.

So there I was at Pad 5, Saturn City.
Saturn City is the hub. From there you can
reach most of the known planets. I pulled out
my phone and looked at the mug shot of my
latest target. I had to find him and put him
back in prison where he belonged.

The Perp was a class A scumbag by the name of Zab Hekko, an ugly slab of pure evil.

I looked at the face on the screen. I saw grey skin. He had two sets of jaws with needle teeth. He had the eyes of a bug and a nose like an elephant's trunk. I tried to picture the lady this freak was dating!

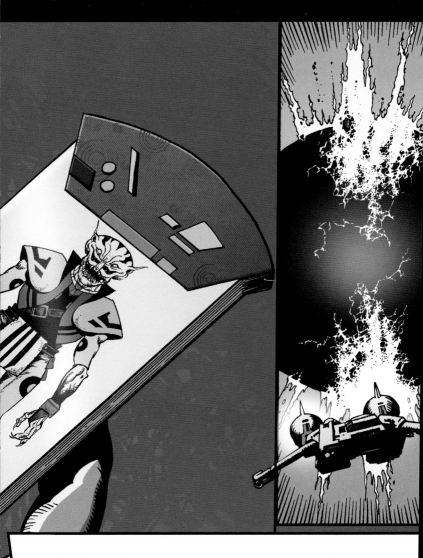

I had put Hekko away five years back. Hekko's the worst kind of bug terrorist. A cop had arrested him, so he had blown up the guy's home planet. I'd call that over the top.

At the time I told myself his life of crime was over. Then a prison guard took a bribe and Hekko went over the wall.

It was bad enough that he had escaped.
A few days later the news got even worse.
Hekko had broken into a lab somewhere.
It was top secret. He got away with a virus
that could wipe out a whole planet. Now he
was going home.

To my home. Planet Earth had tried to lock
him away, so planet Earth had to be destroyed.
That was his mission.

Yes, Hekko was on his way to Earth, my wonderful blue and green planet of twenty billion people. I had to take him out before he took out the human race. It was as simple as that. If that virus got in the air, twenty billion people would die. This was a job for one guy. Me. I knew Hekko. I knew what made him tick.

But I had a problem. The cops in Saturn City had taken a call. It was from the wife of this plastic surgeon. Her husband had done a face job on a freak with grey skin, needle teeth, bug eyes and a nose like a trunk. It was Hekko. Guess what? The doctor had just turned up dead and Hekko had a new face. He could look like you. He could look like me.

Bummer.

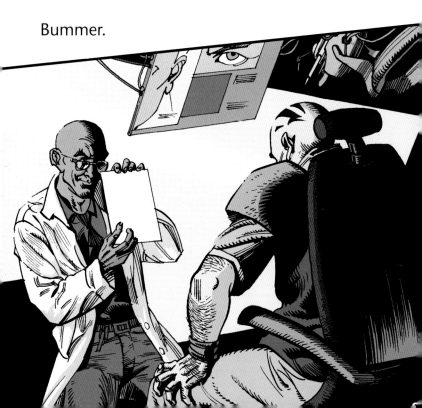

CHAPTER 2

The shuttle to Earth was like a city in space. It carried ten thousand people. It was the biggest spaceship in the galaxy. Hekko was on board somewhere, but how was I going to find him? I watched the crowd. Even half empty, the shuttle made my job hard.

Like I said. Bummer.

I found my seat, put on my belt and took
a pill to stop my ears and eyes popping.
The take-off was something else. It felt like
a hand had reached inside and flipped me
inside out. But it didn't take long before I felt
human again and went looking for my man.
The journey to Earth only took three days.
I had to work fast.

I spent day one getting used to the place. On day two I got down to work. I walked through the food hall. I went in the gym and the shopping mall. Last stop was the pool hall. It was bad guy heaven. One or two of the punters knew me. I knew them. They put down their cues and left.

The crowd got thin and I spotted somebody
I knew: a gunrunner by the name of Venda Lap
Jin. She sold shooters to anyone who wanted
them. She had done time for murder. I had
almost been one of her victims. One time, she
put a shot in my shoulder. I put two in her
head. Lucky for her she had two heads!

OK, so what was she doing here? Of all the places in all the galaxy she had to walk in here. Why? I got a funny feeling. This wasn't chance. No way. She and Hekko had done time in the same prisons. She was here because of him. They were a team. They were working together. I would bet my life on it. Come to think of it, I just had …

Was I going to come out of this alive? The odds weren't good.

I pushed through the crowd. She didn't see me until it was too late.

"Hi, Venda," I said.

I already had my hand on my gun. I saw her eyes go wide, all three of them. Her mouth dropped open. Then her other mouth did the same. She went for her gun. I went for mine. I was too quick. I drew my gun first.

"Don't do it, Venda," I said. "You don't want me to spoil your pretty little faces."

She looked. She thought. She put the gun down.

"Clever girl," I said. "Now where is he?"

"Where's who?"

"Don't act stupid," I told her.

I saw her hand creeping to a pocket. Was it another gun? Then I understood. It was her phone. She was trying to warn Hekko.

I hit her hand with my gun. I heard the bones crack. She yelped with pain. I took the phone and went through her contacts. There he was: Zab Hekko, bug terrorist. There was a face ID. He looked human.

"He got a good face job," I said. "But he's still the same scumbag underneath."

I saw two cops walk in. I flashed my ID.

"Take her away," I said. "I'm going after her boss."

CHAPTER 3

I looked hard at the face ID. I put the new Hekko in my memory: the black hair, the yellow and still buggy eyes, the square jaw. I went on my way. Where was he? I searched the sports halls. I tried the computer lounge. Nothing. There was no way I could go through ten thousand bedrooms. What could I do?

Then I got lucky. Venda's phone went. It was him. He was trying to call her. I didn't answer. I ran a trace on the call. He was on the top deck of the ship. I started to run. I went up the stairs three at a time, pushing past the people coming down.

"Get out of the way!" I yelled.

I flashed my ID.

"Move!"

As I ran, the phone rang again. Hekko wanted to know where Venda was.

I had to get there fast before he went on the run. I went through the sliding doors. The top deck had a curved, glass roof. There was a great view of deep space, but I wasn't looking. I only had eyes for Hekko. I looked left. I looked right. The place was vast. Where did I start?

I moved into the crowd. There were hundreds of people looking up at the stars. I had my hand on my gun. My heart was thudding. I could feel the sweat on my back.

It was like this: Hekko had a deadly virus in a ball of glass. What if he broke it? If it could kill millions in days, it could kill thousands in seconds. Everybody on board would die.

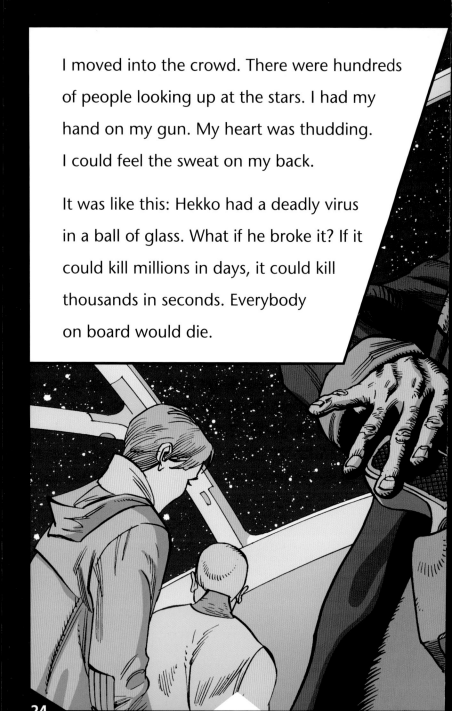

I was still looking for Hekko when my phone went. It was the head of security.

"Kade?" he asked.

"Yes?"

"It's Venda. She killed the cops. She's coming your way."

I switched off the phone. Then I heard a yell.

"Hekko!"

Venda was screaming a warning at somebody.

I saw a head turn. It was him. A hard arrest had just got harder. Venda was making me work. She was coming through the door pointing the gun she had taken from one of the dead cops. Hekko was turning, drawing his own weapon.

CHAPTER 4

Venda was the main danger. I had to take her out. I squeezed the trigger. Her head exploded. It was the only good one she had left. I spun round, turning my gun on Hekko. I saw him smile. He was holding a glass ball in his right hand.

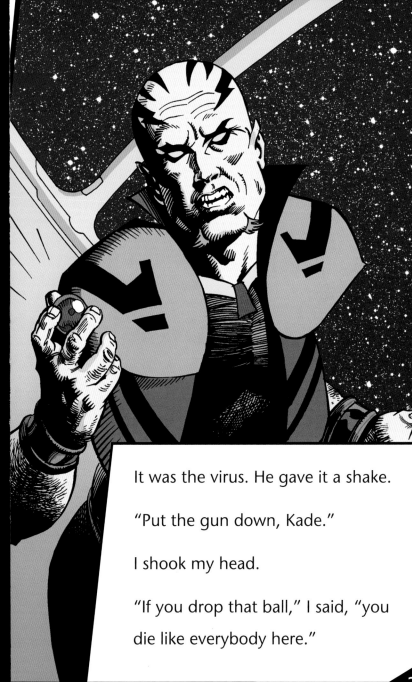

It was the virus. He gave it a shake.

"Put the gun down, Kade."

I shook my head.

"If you drop that ball," I said, "you die like everybody here."

It was a stupid thing to say. People started to scream. They ran in panic.

"You're wrong, Kade," Hekko said with a smile on his face. "This virus kills *people*. Maybe you forgot: I'm not human."

Then he tossed the ball in the air.

At the same time he pulled his gun
and started to shoot. He blew a hole in a
waiter. The guy was in the wrong place at the
wrong time. He shot out a huge glass window.
I was running. I only had one go at this. I threw
myself on the floor, skidding across the tiles.

With my left hand, I caught the ball.

With my right hand, I fired.

The ball was OK.

Hekko wasn't OK. He lay on the ground screaming. It was a good shot. He had lost his hand, but he was still alive. I was still shaking as I walked over to him. I looked down.

"You're finished, bug boy," I told him.

He didn't answer. He was still screaming. Two cops arrived.

"Cuff him," I said.

The cops stared at the missing hand. I laughed.

"Don't worry, guys," I said. "You'll think of something."

CHAPTER 5

I found my room and put the ball in the safe.
I lay on the bed. I was going to book a holiday.
I needed a good, long rest.

Half an hour later my phone went. It was
my boss.

"Kade?"

"Yes."

"I've got a job for you."

I listened to her for a few minutes. A gang of outlaws from Neptune had kidnapped some zillionaire's kid.

The holiday was on hold.

Reader challenge

Word hunt

1 On page 10, find a word made of two words.

2 On page 18, find a verb that means "sneaking".

3 On page 23, find a word that means "very large".

Story sense

4 What did Kade do to Venda? (page 28)

5 Why couldn't the virus kill Hekko? (page 30)

6 How did Kade stop the ball from smashing? (pages 32–33)

7 How did Kade stop Hekko in the end?

8 How do you think Kade felt at the end of the story?

Your views

9 Do you think Kade did the right thing by shooting Hekko and Venda? Give reasons.

10 Did you find any parts of the story funny? If so, which parts?

Spell it

With a partner, look at these words and then cover them up.

- crime
- alive
- bribe

Take it in turns for one of you to read the words aloud. The other person has to try and spell each word. Check your answers, then swap over.

Try it

With a partner, read pages 32 and 33 again. Make a freeze-frame of the shooting scene between Kade and Hekko.

William Collins's dream of knowledge for all began with the publication of his first book in 1819. A self-educated mill worker, he not only enriched millions of lives, but also founded a flourishing publishing house. Today, staying true to this spirit, Collins books are packed with inspiration, innovation and practical expertise. They place you at the centre of a world of possibility and give you exactly what you need to explore it.

Collins. Freedom to teach.

Published by Collins Education
An imprint of HarperCollins*Publishers*
77–85 Fulham Palace Road
Hammersmith
London
W6 8JB

Browse the complete Collins Education catalogue at **www.collinseducation.com**

Text by Alan Gibbons and Robbie Gibbons © HarperCollins Publishers Limited 2012
Illustrations © Eoin Coveney 2012

Series consultants: Alan Gibbons and Natalie Packer

10 9 8 7 6 5 4 3 2 1
ISBN 978-0-00-746475-3

British Library Cataloguing in Publication Data.
A catalogue record for this publication is available from the British Library.

Commissioned by Catherine Martin
Edited and project-managed by Sue Chapple
Illustration management by Tim Satterthwaite
Proofread by Grace Glendinning
Design and typesetting by Jordan Publishing Design Limited
Cover design by Paul Manning

Acknowledgements

The publishers would like to thank the students and teachers of the following schools for their help in trialling the Read On series:

Southfields Academy, London
Queensbury School, Queensbury, Bradford
Langham C of E Primary School, Langham, Rutland
Ratton School, Eastbourne, East Sussex
Northfleet School for Girls, North Fleet, Kent
Westergate Community School, Chichester, West Sussex
Bottesford C of E Primary School, Bottesford, Nottinghamshire
Woodfield Academy, Redditch, Worcestershire
St Richard's Catholic College, Bexhill, East Sussex